THE ONLY CHILD CLUB

Mr Adulewebe   Ryan

Tasha   Oliver   Jade

Books by Anne Fine

Care of Henry

Nag Club

*How to Cross the Road
and Not Turn into a Pizza*

The Haunting of Pip Parker

The Jamie and Angus Stories

Jamie and Angus Together

Jamie and Angus Forever

Under a Silver Moon

The Party Club

THE ONLY CHILD CLUB

ANNE FINE

Illustrated by Arthur Robins

WALKER BOOKS

First published 2013 by Walker Books Ltd
87 Vauxhall Walk, London SE11 5HJ

This edition published 2014

4 6 8 10 9 7 5 3

Text © 2013 Anne Fine
Illustrations © 2013 Arthur Robins

The right of Anne Fine and Arthur Robins to be identified as
author and illustrator respectively of this work has been asserted by
them in accordance with the Copyright, Designs and Patents Act 1988

This book has been typeset in Palatino

Printed and bound in Great Britain by Clays Ltd, St Ives plc

British Library Cataloguing in Publication Data:
a catalogue record for this book is available from the British Library

ISBN 978-1-4063-5508-6

www.walker.co.uk

For Johnny

A.F.

For Izzy, then along came Bessy

A.R.

~Chapter One~

The List

Ryan sat at his desk in the classroom.

He was writing very carefully and neatly.

Surina leaned over to look. "Why are you putting down all our names?" she asked.

"I'm making a list," said Ryan. "A list of everyone in our class."

"Why?"

"Because I'm going to start a club."

"What sort of club?"

It's going to be the Only Child Club,

Ryan told her.

Can I join?

she asked him.

I love clubs!

"No," Ryan said.

Surina pointed to her name. "But I'm on your list."

"Everyone's on the list," said Ryan, "because I need to make sure that I haven't forgotten anyone in the class. But lots of them will be crossed off. And you will definitely be crossed off."

Surina

"Why?" asked Surina.

"Because you have brothers and sisters," Ryan explained. He ticked them off on his fingers. "You have a brother in the next class up, and two sisters in the nursery. So you can't join, because this is the Only Child Club. It's for only children."

"Well, boo to you!" said Surina.

Ryan shook his head. "I'm sorry," he told her, "but you're not an only child. So you can't join. And you won't be the only one to be crossed off."

Surina wasn't pleased. She stuck out her tongue. "Well, double boo to you," she told him.

Ryan pretended that he hadn't heard and just carried on with his writing.

~Chapter Two~

Crossing People Off

As soon as the buzzer went for break, Ryan picked up his list and went round the playground, checking to see who could join his club and who would have to be crossed off. Most people got crossed off. Tyler had a sister. So did Teddy and Gurdeep. Nathan had two brothers. Sian had two sisters, two stepsisters and a half-brother. Susie, Emily

and Mandy all had one brother. Matt had

three.

Do babies count? I want to
join but Mum just had a baby.
He doesn't do much except
eat and sleep.
So can I join?

asked Zachary.

"No," Ryan said.

"Oh, go on!" wheedled Zachary. "Just for

now. Just till he starts crawling about and

snatching my stuff, and being a proper

brother."

"No," Ryan told Zachary *Zachary*

firmly. "It wouldn't be right."

And he put a thick black pencil

line through Zachary's name on the list.

Zachary shrugged. "Oh, well." He

looked at all the crossed-off names. "Good

luck in finding someone."

"Thank you," said Ryan, and he carried

on round the playground, holding his list,

looking for the rest of the people in his class.

Patrick wanted to join.

"I'm sorry," Ryan said. "You can't. You're

not an only child. I know you have a sister."

"But I'm adopted," Patrick argued. "And I can't remember back that far, but maybe before I was adopted I was an only child."

"Well, you're not an only child *now*," Ryan said sternly. "You have a brother and a sister in the big school who pick you up every day. So you are definitely not an only child."

Patrick stared at the list. It was plastered with thick black pencil lines. "Who's going to join?" he said. "You've gone round the class and crossed out everyone."

"Not *everyone*," said Ryan. He counted

up. "There are three people not crossed out.

Jade, Oliver and Tasha. And then there's me."

"Four altogether?" scoffed Patrick.

"That's not much of a club."

"That's all right," Ryan said. "We only

children are used to not being in a crowd."

Chapter Three

Jade

Jade didn't want to join.

"I'm busy every break," she said.

"You can be busy in our club,"

Ryan tried to tempt her.

"No," Jade said stubbornly.

"I want to play on the bars.

We're doing double swingers

and I'm the best. I want to stay

the best, and that means

practising and never missing

my turn."

Ryan said, "Are you sure? We only

children ought to stick together."

Jade stared at him. "Why?"

Ryan couldn't think of any answer to

that. So he pretended his shoelace had

come undone and bent to tie it up. He kept

his head down, fiddling with his laces, till

Jade got bored and went back to the swing

bars. Then he crossed Jade's name off the

list, but lightly, in case she

ever changed her mind.

~Chapter Four~

The First Meeting

Ryan and Tasha and Oliver sat on the bench outside the lunch hall. Ryan took charge.

"Right," he said. "This is the very first meeting of the Only Child Club so I think we should make a list of all the things that only children never get to do. And then we can do them."

"All right," said Oliver.

"Good idea," agreed Tasha.

They sat and thought.

"Sharing a bedroom?" suggested Tasha
after a while.

Ryan shook his head. "No. That won't do.
I have to share my bedroom a lot. I have to
share it every time my cousins come to stay,
and that's quite often."

"I have to share mine, too," admitted Oliver.
"I have a lot of sleepovers with Tyler and
Gurdeep. And when my Aunt May comes,
she sleeps in my bed and I have a little

 blow-up bed on the floor."

"All right," said Ryan. "We'll think of something else."

"Having someone to play games with?" said Oliver.

The other two shook their heads. "No," Tasha said. "All of us play with other people all the time in school."

"We have friends over, too," added Ryan, "and you have just admitted you have a lot of sleepovers with Tyler and Gurdeep. I bet you play then."

"We do," said Oliver. "We play until we get told off."

Tasha said, "Rupinder next door helped me make a hole in the fence. And my mum says I spend more time playing in their garden now than I do in my own. So I have someone to play games with after school as well."

"Me too," said Oliver. "I play with Colin up the street. And every Tuesday, Lucy from nursery gets dropped off at my house before school so that her mum can start work early." He blushed. "We usually play Bears and Wolves."

"There you go," Ryan said, sighing. "We

all have someone to play games with. So that idea won't do."

"No," the other two agreed gloomily. "That idea certainly won't do."

Ryan stood up. "We must go home tonight and think of something before the next meeting. We'll each think of something we've never, ever, ever done because we don't have brothers or sisters. And then we'll do those things and write them on our special Only Child Club list."

"All right," the other two agreed. And they ran back to the playground to play games with their other friends.

~Chapter Five~

Something I've Never,
Ever Done

Ryan came to the next meeting holding a

cereal box. It was brand new. No one had

even opened it at the top. And on the front

it said in spidery letters:

FREE INSIDE!

Your Creepy-Crawly Creature!
Collect the whole set!

 On the back of the box there was a picture of eight different creepy-crawly creatures, all sitting in a circle round a tiny campfire, having a party. A few were black; one was green; two were purple. One or two had spots. Two had feathery feelers. But all of them looked dead creepy and horribly crawly. They all had names.

"Which one do you think is in the packet?" Tasha asked. "I hope it's Doug the Bug. I like him best."

"We won't know till we open it," Ryan reminded her.

 "Well, if it's Doug the Bug, bags I get him," Tasha said.

"You can't just *bags* him," Oliver told her

firmly. "That isn't fair."

"I asked *first*," Tasha insisted.

"Only because you're *rude*,"

said Oliver. "It's Ryan's cereal box."

"If Ryan wanted it, he'd have already

opened the box and taken it out," argued

Tasha. She turned to Ryan. "Wouldn't you?"

"No," Ryan said. "I brought the box along

because we decided to think of something

we've never, ever, ever done because we

don't have brothers and sisters. And one of

the things I've never, ever, ever done is have

a fight about who gets the free

gift in a box of cereal."

"That's a good one," said Oliver. "Neither have I."

"I can't remember if I have," said Tasha. "I probably haven't. But you can give Doug the Bug to me anyway."

"Why?" Ryan asked.

Tasha shrugged. "Because of 'ladies first'?"

"That is ridiculous!" said Ryan. "If we followed that rule, you would get everything."

"Not *everything*. Only things *first*."

"But if there was only one, you'd always be the one to get it!"

"OK by me!"

"But not OK by me!" said Oliver.

"Or me!" said Ryan. "And since it's my

cereal box, I should get the free gift."

Tasha pointed a finger at him. "If you feel that way, you should never have brought the box to school with you!"

"Why not?"

"Because it's *rude*. It's rude and hurtful!"

"I don't see why. I was just doing something we all agreed to do! That's not rude and hurtful!"

Their voices were getting louder and
louder. All the other children gathered round.

"What's going on?" asked Zachary.

"They're quarrelling," explained Gurdeep.
"They're quarrelling over who should get
the free gift in that cereal box."

Everyone sat down in a circle to watch
the quarrel.

"You're being really, really selfish!" Tasha accused Ryan.

Oliver defended him. "He was just trying to be *helpful*."

"Well then, he's stupid!" Tasha said. "He might have known that one free gift can't go round three people!"

"Don't call me stupid!" shouted Ryan.

"I'll call you stupid if I want," Tasha shouted back. "Because you are! You're stupid, stupid, stupid!"

The quarrel went on all through break. Finally the buzzer went. Regretfully everyone stood up and brushed the grit off their clothes, ready to go back to their classrooms.

Ryan snatched up his cereal box and tore it open. He reached inside and felt around. The gift was in a little plastic bag. It turned out to be one of the purple creepy-crawlies. She was called Scary Mary. Ryan offered her to Tasha.

"There you are. She's not as good as Doug the Bug, but no one's lucky all the time."

Tasha said, "But she's yours really. Don't you want her?"

"No," Ryan said. "I have the whole set already. I just wanted to have the quarrel about it."

"Oh!" Tasha said. She turned to Oliver.

"How about you?"

"I'm not collecting them," admitted Oliver.
"I just liked being part of the quarrel too."

They all went into class. Ryan took out
his pencil and the sheet of paper on which
he'd written:

The Special
Only Child Club
List

He put a neat *1* in the margin, and then he
wrote in his best handwriting:

1. Have a quarrel about who should
   get the free gift in the cereal box.

And after that he wrote: Good fun!

~Chapter Six~

Spending the Whole Day Bickering About Nothing

Tasha came in early next morning and dumped her bag on her chair. She went to stand by Ryan at the window while Mr Adulewebe was getting ready to take the register.

"Look," Ryan said. "It's started to rain."

"No, it hasn't," said Tasha.

Ryan gave her a funny look. "Can't you

34

see?" he said. "There are rain spots all over the playground."

"It's probably bird spit," said Tasha.

"That's crazy," said Ryan. He was really staring at her now. "Birds don't spit all together. Those spots are wet from raindrops. And they're getting bigger, and there are more and more of them."

"I don't think so," said Tasha.

"Well, look again!" Ryan ordered. "The playground is getting wet all over. You can *see* the rain coming

down now. And the tarmac has gone all shiny."

"That could be something else," insisted Tasha. "Maybe the caretaker polished the tarmac before school, or something."

Ryan said irritably, "You're talking *rubbish*, Tasha! That's rain, that is! You've seen rain a hundred thousand times before." His voice was getting louder. "You *must* recognize rain!"

Tasha just shook her head. "It doesn't look like rain to me."

Ryan was *infuriated*. "Look! Look! It's all over the windows!" He pointed. "What are

all those little tadpole things running down
the glass, if they're not raindrops?"

"They do look odd," agreed Tasha. "But
I don't think they're raindrops because

it isn't raining."

"It is!"

screamed Ryan.

"Yes, it is!"

Mr Adulewebe

called over. "Hey,

you two! Would

you stop bickering

and go back to your seats, please?"

Ryan scowled horribly at Tasha. Tasha
just smiled and shrugged.

At lunchtime Tasha slid into the queue right

behind Ryan. She heard him ask for pizza, so

she chose exactly the same. She followed him

past Mr Adulewebe, who was on dinner duty.

She waited till Ryan had chosen a table, then

took the chair opposite. She waited till he had

fetched his water and picked up his knife and

fork, and then she leaned over the table.

"Excuse me," she said to Ryan. "You have

the wrong slice of pizza."

Ryan was puzzled.

"Sorry?"

Tasha pointed to

Ryan's plate. "That pizza

is mine." She lifted her own plate. "This one is yours. I've carried it over for you."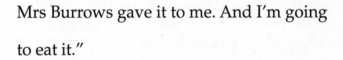

"What are you talking about?" he demanded. "I stood in line for this. Mrs Burrows gave it to me. And I'm going to eat it."

"You can't," she said, "because it's mine."

"How is it *yours*?" snapped Ryan. "It wasn't given to *you*. Mrs Burrows gave it to *me*."

"Yes. But that one should have been *my* slice, and this one should have been yours."

Ryan studied his own slice of pizza, then he inspected Tasha's. "Mine isn't even bigger," he said. "There is no reason on earth why you should want to swap."

"I don't want to swap," said Tasha. "I just want my slice of pizza back." She lifted her plate again. "And you can have *yours*."

Ryan was getting cross now. "So what makes that one *mine*?"

"It just is," Tasha said.

"It's not!"

"Yes, it is."

"It's not!" yelled Ryan. His face was scarlet. "No, it's not! It's not! It's not! *It's not!*"

In the middle of all the yelling, Mr Adulewebe appeared at their table. "Are you two bickering again? Well, you're to stop it. Right now. Do you understand?"

"Yes," Tasha told him cheerfully.

"Yes," Ryan muttered.

"Good," said Mr Adulewebe, "because from now on I shall be watching you both very closely indeed."

He wandered back to his own table.

Ryan gave Tasha his most ferocious look. Tasha just smiled and got on with eating her pizza.

* * *

At going home time, while Ryan was chatting to Oliver in the cloakroom, Tasha appeared at their side.

"Oh, no!" groaned Ryan. "Not you again!"

Tasha smiled at him sweetly. "I've come to do you a favour," she announced. "I've come to tell you that you have your coat on inside out."

Ryan looked down. "No, I haven't."

"You have," she said. "Honestly."

"Look!" He pointed. "See? This is a *pocket*. So my coat's the right way out."

"He's right," said Oliver.

"He's not," said Tasha. "That pocket

ought to be on the inside. He's got the whole thing on wrong."

"I always wear it this way," Ryan said. "This is the way it *came*."

"You've been wearing it wrong all the time, then," she told him.

Ryan said crossly, "This is the way it was hung on the hanger in the shop!"

"I can't help that. You've still got it on all wrong."

"I haven't!"

"Yes, you have."

Ryan was getting louder now. His voice was echoing around the cloakroom. "It's my coat! So I know how to wear it better than you!"

"He's right," said Oliver. "It is his coat. He should know how to wear it."

"Yes!" Ryan shouted. "So leave me alone, Tasha! Just push off home and leave me alone!"

Mr Adulewebe poked his head round the door. "What's all the noise? What's going on here?"

Then he saw Ryan, red-faced, glowering at Tasha.

"You two again!" he said. "I'm fed up with the pair of you. You've spent the whole day bickering about nothing! Well, just go home, both of you. At once!"

Ryan stomped off. Oliver followed him and Tasha ran after them.

"Well, aren't you going to write it on the special Only Child Club list?" she said to Ryan.

"Write down what?" he asked grumpily.

"What Mr Adulewebe said. 'Spending the

45

whole day bickering about nothing.' We

only children *never* get to do that."

Ryan and Oliver stopped and stared at her.

"She's right," said Oliver at last. "We

never get to bicker all day long."

"I suppose not," admitted Ryan. "Either

we're reminded that whoever we're

bickering with is a guest, or they are sent

home early. We get to bicker, but not all

day long."

Tasha hugged herself happily. "I've *always* wanted to do that," she said. "And now I have. And we can put it on the list."

Ryan pulled the sheet of paper out of his pocket and turned to Oliver. "It's just a shame you didn't hear it all, right from the start."

"I heard enough," said Oliver. "All the class heard almost all of it."

So Ryan wrote it on the list:

2. Spend the whole day bickering about nothing.

~Chapter Seven~

Working All Day on Something

The next day, Oliver came in with a lump of modelling clay and lots of matches with their heads cut off.

"What's all that for?" Ryan asked.

"I'm going to make a model of the planets," Oliver said. He ticked them off on his fingers. "Mercury, Venus, Earth, Mars, Jupiter, Saturn, Uranus and Neptune.

And that's in the right order."

Both of them stared at him. "How did you remember that?"

"Easy," said Oliver. He ticked them off again on his fingers. "My Very Educated Mother Just Served Us Noodles."

"What about Pluto?" asked Tasha. "I thought that was a planet too."

"Not any more," said Oliver. "It's been crossed off the list."

"Why?"

But Oliver didn't know. And he was keen to get started, anyway. He pulled lumps off his modelling clay and warmed them up by rolling them round in his hands. Then he bent over his desk and started work.

He worked all day – all through the taking of the register, all through the little breaks between lessons, and all through playtime. He took his models into the lunch hall with him, and carried on working under the table, where no one could see him, while Tasha and Ryan fed him like a baby.

Out in the playground, sitting on the step, Oliver used the matches to hold the tiny thin clay rings he put round Saturn. They were so delicate they kept breaking. It was very difficult. But he kept going, right up until the buzzer went and lessons started again. Later, in story time, he pulled the model out and carried on. Mr Adulewebe saw him, but said he didn't mind because he knew that Oliver was still listening to the story.

Oliver worked on the model all through story time. And when the buzzer sounded

 for the end
of school,
the other two
gathered round.

"Brilliant!" said

Tasha. "Your planets look ultra-good."

"They're perfect," Ryan agreed. "When

I roll clay, it never seems to end up

completely round."

"I love your spindly little rings round

Saturn," Tasha said.

"It wasn't easy," Oliver admitted. "I had

to try a lot of different ways to get them to

stay in place."

The three of them stood quietly for

a little while, admiring the model. Then Oliver said, "Go on, then, Tasha. Knock it onto the floor." He turned to Ryan. "And then you tread on it."

Tasha and Ryan stared.

"I know," said Oliver. "Now come on. Hurry up. The buzzer went ages ago. We ought to go. So, Tasha, you knock it off the desk. And, Ryan, you tread on it."

Tasha spread her hands. "But *why*?" she asked. "Why would you want us to *do* that?"

"It's my choice," Oliver explained. "It's what I want to put on the special Only Child Club list. It's something that everyone in the world with brothers and sisters has done. They've spent the whole day on something, and then some clumsy elephant in the family has come along and knocked it off the shelf, or trodden on it by mistake."

There was a long, long silence. Then Tasha asked him, "Are you *sure*?"

"Yes. I'm sure."

"You won't be cross? You won't burst into tears?"

Oliver told her irritably, "I don't *know*, do I? I am an only child. It's never, ever *happened*. So that's what I want to find out."

"Well," Tasha said dubiously, "if you're *sure*…"

Gently she pushed the model a tiny bit nearer the edge of the desk. Then a tiny bit nearer.

"Oh, hurry up," urged Oliver. "My mum is waiting at the gates.

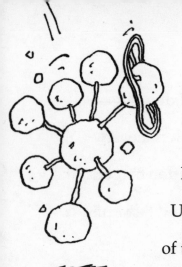

Shutting her eyes, Tasha

gave one more little push.

Neptune tipped over the edge.

Uranus followed, and the two

of them dragged all the other

planets over onto the floor.

Everyone looked down. Saturn's rings

were broken, but most of the rest of the model

looked as if it could be rescued fairly easily.

Oliver turned to Ryan. "Go on, then. Tread

on it."

"It's broken anyway," said Ryan.

"Not enough," said Oliver. "It's not quite

ruined. Hurry up."

Ryan stuck out his foot above the model.

Then, "I *can't*," he said.

"You *have* to," Oliver told him fiercely. "You two both got to put the thing you chose on the special Only Child Club list and this is my choice, so you have to do it."

Like Tasha, Ryan had to close his eyes. Then he took one very long, deep breath and stomped down hard on Oliver's lovely model.

Splat!

Ryan lifted his foot. Underneath lay a puddle of flat clay and broken matchsticks. The model was in ruins. You couldn't even tell what it had been.

Tasha and Ryan watched Oliver closely. First he squeezed his eyes tight, as if he was trying to be upset enough to cry. Next he clenched his fists, as if he was trying to be mad enough to hit someone. Then he opened his mouth wide, as if he was trying to be cross enough to shout really loud.

In the end he just shrugged and put his hands in his pockets.

"I don't really think that I feel much at all," he said.

"Perhaps that's because you knew all along that this was going to happen," suggested Tasha.

"Perhaps," agreed Oliver. "Still, after all that work, it is a *little* disappointing."

"Never mind," Ryan comforted him. "At least it goes on the list."

He drew the sheet of paper out of his pocket and took a pencil off Oliver's desk. In the margin he put a neat 3. And then he wrote, in his best handwriting:

3. Work all day on
    something, only to have
    someone ruin it.

Then they rushed out of the classroom before Oliver's mother could come in to fetch them.

~Chapter Eight~

The End of
the Only Child Club

Next morning, Ryan called a special

meeting of the Only Child Club. The three

of them sat in a corner of the playground,

privately, before the first buzzer rang.

"We're closing down," he told them.

"I think we've done everything we can do."

Tasha studied the list.

1. Have a quarrel about who should get the free gift in the cereal box.

2. Spend the whole day bickering about nothing.

3. Work all day on something, only to have someone ruin it.

"The first was quite fun," she said. "And I enjoyed the one I chose too."

"But mine didn't work too well," said Oliver. "And I can't think of anything else."

"Neither can I," said Ryan. "Almost everything else, you can do with your friends and your cousins."

Tasha pointed to the list. "You could probably even do those three with good friends or cousins who stayed with you quite a lot."

"I think you could." Ryan stood up. "I now declare the Only Child Club closed," he said. And to prove it, he tore up the list and  shoved the pieces in the litter bin.

Jade came in through the gates and saw them standing in their little group, wondering what to do next. "Are you still busy with your club?" she said to Tasha.

"No," Tasha told her. "That's all finished now."

"Good!" Jade said. "Want to come with me and practise double swingers on the bars?"

"Yes, please," said Tasha. And the two of them linked arms and skipped away.

Oliver turned to Ryan. "Fancy a race to the climbing frame?"

"Bet you I win!" said Ryan.

And they both ran off.

Anne Fine is a distinguished writer for adults and children. She has won many awards for her children's books, including the Carnegie Medal twice, the Whitbread Children's Book of the Year Award twice, the Smarties Book Prize and the Guardian Children's Fiction Prize. In 2001, Anne became Children's Laureate and in 2003, she was awarded an OBE. Anne has two grown-up daughters and lives in County Durham.

Arthur Robins has illustrated numerous children's books and exhibited his work in London. He has won a Gold Award in the Nestlé Smarties Book Prize and a Design & Art Direction Silver Award. In 2001, he illustrated the Royal Mail Christmas stamps. Arthur lives in Surrey.

You can find out more about Anne Fine and Arthur Robins by visiting their websites at **www.annefine.co.uk** and **www.artrobins.com**